This Little Tiger book belongs to:

_____

_____

_____

To Fred, George and Thomas, my pirates in pyjamas,

and Christopher – the captain of our ship

~ C C

For Archie, Seth and Tabby

~ T K

LITTLE TIGER PRESS
1 The Coda Centre
189 Munster Road, London SW6 6AW
www.littletiger.co.uk

First published in Great Britain 2015
Text copyright © Caroline Crowe 2015
Illustrations copyright © Tom Knight 2015
Caroline Crowe and Tom Knight have asserted their rights
to be identified as the author and illustrator of this work
under the Copyright, Designs and Patents Act, 1988
A CIP catalogue record for this book
is available from the British Library
All rights reserved

ISBN 978-1-84869-136-0
Printed in China
LTP/1400/1147/0515
2 4 6 8 10 9 7 5 3 1

Pirates in Pyjamas

Caroline Crowe

Tom Knight

LITTLE TIGER PRESS

London

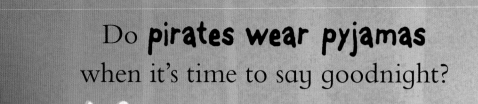

Do **pirates wear pyjamas**
when it's time to say goodnight?

TREASURE ISLAND
Robert Louis Stevenson

Do they have a skull and crossbones,
are they **stripy, black** and **white?**

No! When pirates choose pyjamas
they're not always what you'd think,
Some are **purple**,

some are **orange**,

some are **yellow, green** and **pink!**

There are knitted ones with **pom-poms**,

ones with **spots** and **frilly sleeves**,

Some are **fluffy** all-in-onesies,

and some finish at the **knees**.

If you board the *Leaky Parrot*
just before you go to bed,
Captain Grotbeard's wearing arm bands,
and a snorkel on his head!

His crew are making shark fins
with the shampoo in their hair.

Fancy Hair Oil

AYE AYE WAX

Finest eye patch polish

BOOTY BUBBLES

Grab your towels!

the Captain cries.

"And dry behind your knees."

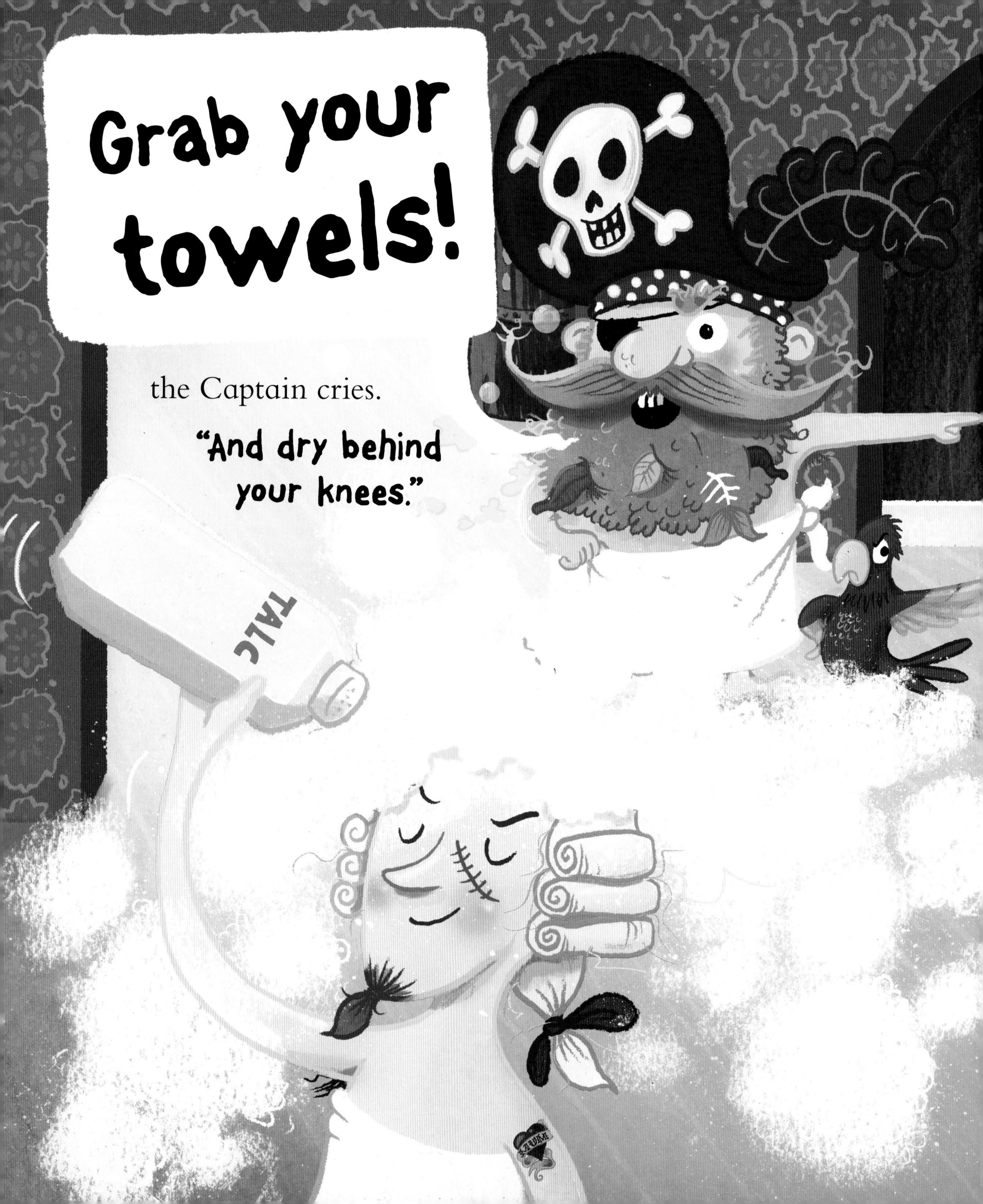

TALC

"The last one in pyjamas smells of **stinky, mouldy cheese!**"

Rotten Roger's jim-jam top has cherry buns and lollies,

and **Hairy Hank's**
   have brollies.

Sneaky Pete's
   have dancing cats,

Captain Grotbeard's onesie,
must have shrunk a size or two,

He can't do up the buttons,
and his **tummy's
poking
through!**

Pirates throw pyjama parties
nearly every single night,
They parade their **jazzy jim-jams**
and have pirate . . .

...pillow fights!

Wallop, whack, white feathers fly,
and tickle everywhere.
Hank laughs so hard, his jim-jams slip . . .

. . . and leave his **bottom** bare!

Dressed for bed, they drink their milk
through **curly whirly** straws.

Then tucked up tight, they rock the ship . . .

...with peaceful
pirate
snores.

Zzzzzz

Zzzzzz

Zzzzzz

So if you want to be a pirate,
you don't need a patch or sword.

You just need your **best pyjamas,** and a **bed** to climb aboard.

More exciting books from Little Tiger Press!

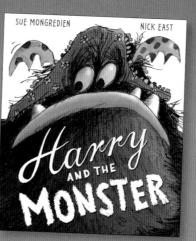

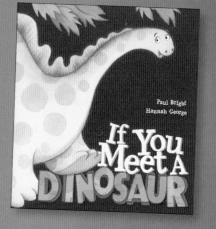

For information regarding any of the above titles or for our catalogue, please contact us:
Little Tiger Press, 1 The Coda Centre, 189 Munster Road, London SW6 6AW
Tel: 020 7385 6333 • Fax: 020 7385 7333 • E-mail: contact@littletiger.co.uk • www.littletiger.co.uk